Acting Edition

Mrs. Kemble's Tempest

by Tom Ziegler

SAMUEL FRENCH

No one shall make any changes in this title(s) for the purpose of production. No part of this book may be reproduced, stored in a retrieval system, scanned, uploaded, or transmitted in any form, by any means, now known or yet to be invented, including mechanical, electronic, digital, photocopying, recording, videotaping, or otherwise, without the prior written permission of the publisher. No one shall share this title(s), or any part of this title(s), through any social media or file hosting websites.

For all inquiries regarding motion picture, television, online/digital and other media rights, please contact Concord Theatricals Corp.

MUSIC AND THIRD-PARTY MATERIALS USE NOTE

Licensees are solely responsible for obtaining formal written permission from copyright owners to use copyrighted music and/or other copyrighted third-party materials (e.g. artworks, logos) in the performance of this play and are strongly cautioned to do so. If no such permission is obtained by the licensee, then the licensee must use only original music and materials that the licensee owns and controls. Licensees are solely responsible and liable for clearances of all third-party copyrighted materials, including without limitation music, and shall indemnify the copyright owners of the play(s) and their licensing agent, Concord Theatricals Corp., against any costs, expenses, losses and liabilities arising from the use of such copyrighted third-party materials by licensees. For music, please contact the appropriate music licensing authority in your territory for the rights to any incidental music.

IMPORTANT BILLING AND CREDIT REQUIREMENTS

If you have obtained performance rights to this title, please refer to your licensing agreement for important billing and credit requirements.

MRS. KEMBLE'S TEMPEST was developed in workshops at Mill Mountain Theatre in Roanoke, Virginia, and Shenandoah Valley International Playwrights Retreat in Verona, Virginia. The cast was as follows:

FANNY KEMBLE . . . . Jane Ridley
THE PETULANT PIANIST . . . . Josh Harvey

DEVELOPMENT OF THE PLAY

For several summers I was invited to participate in the Shenandoah International Playwrights' Retreat, also known as ShenanArts, in Verona, VA. One of the plays I worked on there, *Grace and Glorie*, went on to be produced in New York and through it I met Estelle Parsons, who suggested that I write a one-woman show. She recommended a book about five famous women, one of whom was Fanny Kemble. After doing much research on Fanny, I decided that the best approach to tell her story was through Shakespeare. After going through all of his plays, I decided that *The Tempest* best correlated with her life.

At the playwright's retreat, there was a stable of actors, directors, and producers available to view the work in progress and make suggestions. One of the regular actors, Jane Ridley, who was actually from England, served as Fanny throughout the development of the play. Hearing my words as spoken by her was very helpful. The first few readthroughs were quite long, and I learned that I would have to speak economically. For one of the "performances" Paul Hilderbrand, one of the founders of ShenanArts, offered to play incidental music to go along with the reading, and in so doing, he inspired the birth of the "Petulant Pianist," who is an integral part of the show. Robert Small and Kathleen Tosco, the other cofounders of the retreat, were also very supportive of the play.

Jere Hodgin, managing director of Mill Mountain Theatre in Roanoke, VA, directed the first few actual productions of the play, even going with it to the Edinburgh Fringe Festival. In Roanoke, Kevin Jones served as the Petulant Pianist. Early in the life of the play, Josh Harvey became the piano player, and he actually wrote out a musical score to accompany the script.

CHARACTERS

FANNY KEMBLE – Fifty-nine, author, reader, and actress

THE PETULANT PIANIST – A Victorian virtuoso

SETTING

Philadelphia on an unusually warm spring evening.

On the dais of an assembly hall, we find, left, a carved, walnut lectern; right, a period side chair and low table; further right, a large Victorian piano. A library table up center flaunts a huge, overly-designed floral arrangement in a large, florid vase, decorated with a massive, gaudy bow. Behind the table stands a framed, red velour screen.

TIME

Evening in 1869.

AUTHOR'S NOTES

This is a two character play: **MRS. KEMBLE** and **THE PIANIST**. Although Mrs. Kemble has all the lines, The Pianist is her worthy collaborator.

The performance time of the play is approximately ninety minutes with no intermission.

Music

Most of the piano selections used in this play are from the work of Felix Mendelssohn and Arthur Sullivan. Mendelssohn and Fanny Kemble were good friends from the time they were teenagers. Arthur Sullivan, shortly before he teamed up with W. S. Gilbert, played the organ at the wedding of Fanny's daughter.

Sheet music for the music in the show is available for a fee. Contact your licensing representative for more information.

FANNY [FRANCES ANN] KEMBLE (1809–1893)

The biography of Fanny Kemble, the nineteenth-century British whirlwind, reads like page one of *The National Enquirer*. Teenage starlet, millionaire's bride, social maverick, notorious divorcée, feminist, abolitionist, Civil War mover and shaker...all at a time when the activities of most women were limited to the kitchen, nursery, and laundry room.

Fanny Kemble was born in 1809 into the foremost acting dynasty of the Georgian stage. Her father, Charles Kemble, was both a famous leading man of the day and manager of London's esteemed Covent Garden Theatre; her mother, Swiss-born Marie-Thérèse de Camp, had been a popular actress, dancer, and musical comedy star.

Her uncle, John Phillip Kemble, and her aunt, Mrs. Sarah Siddons, were among the greatest Shakespearean actors of all time.

Educated in France, Fanny returned home an accomplished writer fluent in French, German, and Italian. The young lady had hoped to begin a career as an author, but in a last-ditch attempt to save himself from bankruptcy, Charles Kemble drafted his nineteen-year-old daughter into the family business.

In the autumn of 1829, Fanny appeared as Juliet before a packed house at Covent Garden in Shakespeare's greatest love story. And she became an overnight sensation.

Much like celebrities today, fans collected her picture, mimicked her hairstyles, and followed details of her personal life in the British and American press. Thus making her, arguably, the first superstar of the entertainment world.

Her father's financial woes persisted, and in 1832 Charles persuaded Fanny to accompany him on a tour through the United States.

Walt Whitman, writing of Fanny's performance in New York City, said: "Fanny Kemble – nothing finer did ever stage exhibit. She came to give America that young maturity and roseate power in all their forenoon flush. It was my good luck to see her nearly every night she play'd at the old Park."

She went on to appear in Boston, Philadelphia, Baltimore, and Washington, D.C., where she enraptured the likes of Daniel Webster, Chief Justice John Marshall, and President Andrew Jackson.

At the end of the tour she did not return to England as planned. Instead she abandoned her career and country to marry Pierce Butler, a wealthy Philadelphian.

The new Mrs. Butler learned too late that the source of her husband's wealth came from large slave plantations off the coast of Georgia. Although Pierce argued that the slaves were treated humanely, Fanny wanted to see for herself. Visiting the island plantations in 1838, she kept a journal detailing her experience of this "peculiar institution" called slavery.

A year later, when Fanny discovered that Butler had been unfaithful, the couple separated. Exiled from her two daughters, Sarah and Frances Anne, Fanny returned to London, where she accepted an offer to perform with William Macready in a series of Shakespeare's plays.

Following her divorce from Pierce Butler in 1849, Fanny returned to America to be close to her children.

Rather than go back to the stage to support herself, she began giving dramatic readings of William Shakespeare's plays. Tickets cost one dollar and netted the now middle-aged divorcée a very substantial income.

Numerous eyewitness accounts of Mrs. Kemble's readings comment that even in complicated scenes, the separate characters were as well differentiated as though they had come onstage as individual actors. One London critic commented: "The detail of each scene was given so naturally that the audience were hardly aware they had not before them the whole *mise en scène*."

That her readings were complex, sophisticated, and intelligent is without question. When James Fenimore Cooper, America's most famous curmudgeon, went to hear Fanny read *The Tempest*, he said, "I have not been so amused by a play since I was a boy." Henry Longfellow was so overwhelmed by her skill he wrote her a sonnet which concluded with:

> O happy Poet! By no critic vext!
> How must thy listening spirit now rejoice
> To be interpreted by such a voice!

A lifelong devotee of the latest in fashion, Fanny is credited at this time as one of the first women ever to wear the scandalous costume called "bloomers."

From riding on the first steam locomotive with George Stephenson to swapping poetry with Alfred Tennyson; from reading Shakespeare to the music of her friend, Felix Mendelssohn to arguing politics over dinner with President Andrew Jackson – Fanny traveled in the highest social and artistic circles.

Few people have left so rich an account of themselves. From the age of seventeen, her record of her travels and observations later became the source of her best-selling memoirs.

This treasure trove of frank, honest, moving, and often humorous reminiscences makes Fanny Kemble a first rate witness to the burgeoning Industrial Revolution and the emergence of Western democracy.

She published her most lasting work, *Journal of a Residence on a Georgian Plantation*, during the Civil War to influence the British opinion against throwing in with the Confederacy. Many historians believe she succeeded.

What set Fanny Kemble apart from the vast majority of Victorian women in both Britain and America was her ability to earn large sums of money. Sums most men could never dream of. She was a shrewd businesswoman; employed loyal agents and managers who arranged for her performances and invested her income. By the time Fanny retired she had single-handedly amassed enough to allow her to live in quiet luxury for the remainder of her life.

Henry James – who credits Fanny with giving him the story for his novel, *Washington Square* – remarked at her funeral: "From first to last Fanny Kemble abundantly lived. With her wonderful air of smouldering embers under ashes, she leaves a great image – a great memory."

(We'll never know what Mrs. Kemble said to her piano accompanist moments before the commencement of her reading of The Tempest. *Whatever it was, she certainly irritated the gentleman.)*

(When he's called to the stage, **THE PIANIST** *enters. His cheeks abristle with pork chop sideburns and he's dressed in black tails, tie, and a waistcoat. He bows curtly to the audience, sits at the piano, and plays the introductory selection,* **[MUSIC 01 – RETURN TO ME, AH BROTHER DEAR]**. *His vexation is evident in the music.)*

(At the conclusion, he turns the page roughly and begins Arthur Sullivan's **[MUSIC 01a – COME UNTO THESE YELLOW SANDS]**, *again with the same ill-tempered expression.)*

*(***FANNY*** enters briskly. She's wearing an exquisite blue gown, stunning jewels, and carries an immense, leather-bound folio of Shakespeare's plays. Acknowledging the audience's applause by curtsying deeply, she stands – with some difficulty – and glances at* **THE PIANIST**. *He looks away. Back stiff, nose elevated.)*

*(***FANNY*** turns to the audience.)*

FANNY. Ladies and Gentlemen. For more than twenty years now, following my forced retirement from... *marriage*...I have traveled through America and Great Britain, earning my livelihood presenting readings of William Shakespeare's plays.

FANNY. Unfortunately – although I have fled mortality with Spartan zeal – I find it ever more difficult to portray adequately the genius contained in these words. Which is why with the conclusion of tonight's performance, I shall bid you and the theatrical profession adieu.

> (**THE PIANIST** *glances at her briefly, turns away.*)

Many of you will no doubt wonder if there is some significance in my making this announcement here in Philadelphia, the "City of Brotherly Love." Indeed.

> (*As she turns and places the book on the lectern, she stops, almost startled.*)

Good heavens! I am sorry, but over the years I have permitted myself "upstaged" by William Macready, Charles Kemble, indeed, by Queen Victoria herself. But never by such a garish display of...

> (*Seizing the vase she marches to the edge of the screen.*)

I don't mean to be troublesome, but wouldn't these be much more at home in some nice Bohemian mortuary? Hello?

> (*When no stagehand appears to fetch the offending arrangement, she turns to* **THE PIANIST** *and thrusts the vase into his hands.*)

> (**THE PIANIST** *– stunned, mortified, enraged – stands and marches off.* **FANNY** *turns to the audience.*)

Oh dear, I can see the headlines in tomorrow's newspapers: "UNFEELING FANNY BANISHES BOUQUET." You Americans are so easily set ablaze. It's the weather here. In my country, in England, the climate – like her population – is temperate, dependable; yes, even stodgy. But in America… This morning for example, a half-inch frost covered the entire landscape. Now, only hours later, here we are gathered, like the ingredients in some stew, simmering in our own juice!

Oh no! Now tomorrow's papers will cry, "FANNY FLOGS PHILADELPHIA'S CLIMATE!"

Believe me, I had never intended to lead such a newsworthy life. Heredity, that is my undoing; born as I was to a long line of Irish actors. Look at my family tree and you'll see: the branches are all straining toward the footlights!

> (**THE PIANIST** *marches back on, goes to his piano, and sits facing off.* **FANNY** *continues with the audience.*)

My father ruled the London stage. My mother once performed for the Emperor of Austria. But the reigning monarch of my pedigree, the most celebrated tragedienne of all time, was my aunt, Mrs. Siddons, Mrs. Sarah "Kemble" Siddons. Whom, I might add…

> (**THE PIANIST** *suddenly taps a high note on the piano.* **FANNY** *stops. Turns to him. He sits there wearing a smug, "Let's get on with it" expression.* **FANNY** *represses her irritation and crosses to the lectern.*)

Ladies and Gentlemen, I am honored to represent for you my favorite of William Shakespeare's masterpieces: *The Tempest.* First performed for King James at the Palace at Whitehall on Hollowmass night in the year, Sixteen Hundred and Eleven, the play remains, two hundred and fifty-eight years later, as nimble as the day it was written.

> (*Opening the book.*)

FANNY. This is the Poet's final play. *His* Farewell. A musical review of all his favorite characters: kings and lovers, monsters and clowns. The setting is right here, the stage itself, this enchanted island set apart from the real world. And in one final fanfare of illusionary brilliance, Mr. Shakespeare gives us another sorcerer in the final display of his powers of illusion...

> *(Creating a distinct voice and a physical bearing for each character.)*

(PROSPERO). Prospero, deposed Duke of Milan...

FANNY. Who is marooned these twelve years on an enchanted isle with...

(MIRANDA). His lovely daughter, Miranda.

FANNY. Now fifteen. Duke and daughter, the island's only human inhabitants, are served by...

(ARIEL). Ariel. A magical sprite...

(CALIBAN). Caliban, an enslaved monster!

FANNY. One day a ship passes bearing a party of noblemen back to Italy: Here is...

(ALONZO). Alonzo, King of Naples...

FANNY. ...together with his son...

(FERDINAND). Ferdinand!

FANNY. These are joined by the King's evil brother...

(SEBASTIAN). ...Sebastian...

FANNY. And his *very* old counselor...

(GONZALO). ...Gon...zal...o.

FANNY. Now pray note. Here is the very man who deposed Prospero. His own brother...

(ANTONIO). *(With a sneer.)* Antonio!

FANNY. Such serious characters. Fortunately, for mirth and merriment we have...

(TRINCULO). *(Cockney accent.)* Trinculo, a fainthearted jester...

(STEPHANO). *(Scottish accent.)* Stephano, a butler with a talent for intoxication!

FANNY. Add to these a crew of sailors, various lords and spirits, and we have a most striking cast of characters.

(Reading.)

Act One, Scene One. On a storm-tossed ship at sea.

(THE PIANIST *launches the thundering* **[MUSIC 02 – STORM MUSIC]***;* **FANNY** *adds the roiling waves, howling wind, and crackles of lightning. She reads:)*

Enter a master and a boatswain.

(Trying to speak above the storm.)

(MASTER). Boatswain!

(BOATSWAIN). Here, master: what cheer?

(MASTER). Speak to the mariners: fall to't, yarely, or we run ourselves aground!

(BOATSWAIN). Heigh, my hearts! Take in the topsail. Tend to the master's whistle. Blow, till thou burst thy wind!

FANNY. Antonio and old Gonzalo enter.

(ANTONIO). Where is the master, boatswain?

(BOATSWAIN). You mar our labor: keep to your cabins!

(GONZALO). Remember whom thou hast aboard.

(BOATSWAIN). What care these roarers for the name of king?

FANNY. A cry within.

(PERSON WITHIN). *(Cupping her mouth with her hands.)* AAAAAH!

(MARINERS). All lost! To prayers, to prayers! All lost!

(GONZALO). Now would I give a thousand furlongs of sea for an acre of barren ground. The wills above be done! But I would fain die a dry death.

*(**FANNY** begins to cough. The piano stops.)*

FANNY. Please forgive me. I'm afraid I shall die a dry death. This room is insufferable. Is it not possible to extinguish those hissing gas lanterns, perhaps throw open a window?

Inasmuch as we've stopped, you undoubtedly have noticed that certain lines from tonight's play – it breaks my heart to say – have been cruelly sacrificed to the exigencies of performance. Over the years I have found it necessary to compress the plays into the measure of my listeners' *short*-suffering capacity. My father, who read from this selfsame book –

*(Again, **THE PIANIST** prods with a high note.)*

(To the audience.) We seem to be accompanied by an "Impatient Pianist" this evening, don't we?

*(**FANNY** reads.)*

Scene Two: On the island before the cave.

(THE PIANIST *plays distant storm music* **[MUSIC 03 – PROSPERO'S ENTRANCE].***)*

Prospero, wearing his magic cloak, enters with Miranda.

(MIRANDA). If by your art, my dearest father, you have
Put the wild waters in this roar, allay them.
O, I have suffered with those that I saw suffer:
a brave vessel dash'd all to pieces.

(PROSPERO). Be collected: I have done nothing but in
care of thee. 'Tis time I should inform
thee farther. Lend thy hand, and pluck my magic
garment from me. Canst thou remember
a time before we came unto this isle?

(MIRANDA). 'Tis far off and rather like a dream than an
assurance.

(PROSPERO). Twelve year since, Miranda, Thy father was
the Duke of Milan and a prince of power, and thou his
only heir and princess no worse issued.

(MIRANDA). O the heavens! What foul play
had we, that we came from thence?

(PROSPERO). *(Becoming agitated.)* My brother and thy
uncle, call'd Antonio –
he whom I loved and to him put the manage
of my state as at that time I was rapt
in secret studies. I pray thee, mark me!
In my false brother awaked an evil nature;

(Growing louder and more agitated.)

and he confederates with The King of Naples,
an enemy to me inveterate! DOST THOU HEAR?!

(MIRANDA). Your tale, sir, would cure deafness!

(PROSPERO). Whereon, one midnight they hurried us
aboard a rotten carcass of a boat, not rigg'd, nor
tackle...sail, nor mast...the very rats instinctively had
quit it. There they hoist us, to cry to the sea that roar'd
to us, to sigh...

(She coughs.)

FANNY. *(To the audience.)* Forgive me.

(Back to the book.)

(MIRANDA). How came we here ashore?

(PROSPERO). By Providence divine. Here on this island we arrived; and here have I, thy schoolmaster...

(Once again she begins to cough.)

FANNY. I'm so sorry.

(Marches to the edge of the screen and calls off.)

Excuse me? Hello?

We, too, seem to have been cast adrift.

(Crossing to **THE PIANIST**.*)*

Would you kindly *fetch* me a small quantity of water?

*(***THE PIANIST*** doesn't move.* **FANNY** *snarls.)*

Please.

*(***THE PIANIST*** rises and goes off.* **FANNY** *waits for him to leave then turns down to chat quietly with the audience.)*

Whenever I read of Prospero, with his wooden staff, tutoring Miranda, I can't help but picture "Madame Faudier" and that bâton she always carried.

It was my mother, you see! Determined that I be spared the actor's lot... when was this? 1816. Off I go, seven years old, across the Channel to Madame Faudier's School for Girls in Boulogne. I can still hear Madame screaming after me, "Cette diable de Kemble!" And I was a devil, too!

Until, at twelve, when I moved on to Paris. Four glorious years, immersed in Voltaire, Rousseau, Madame de Staël, Hugo. I returned home thoroughly awash in...

(Marching across the stage.)

Liberté! Egalité! Fraternité!

> *(And directly into the scowl of her disapproving* **PIANIST**, *who stands there holding a pitcher of water and a glass.)*

Back so soon.

> *(A small curtsy as she takes the pitcher and glass.)*

Merci.

> *(Sipping the water, she sets the pitcher and glass on the side table.)*

Miranda was speaking, was she not?

> *(Returning to the book.)*

(**MIRANDA**). And now, I pray you, sir,
For still 'tis beating in my mind, your reason
For raising this sea-storm?

(**PROSPERO**). Know thus far forth. By accident most strange,
bountiful Fortune, now my dear lady, hath
mine enemies brought to this shore!

> *(**FANNY** turns to* **THE PIANIST**. *The gentleman, lost in his distress, has missed a cue.)*

Enter Ariel?

> *(**THE PIANIST** sits up, plays* **[MUSIC 04 – ARIEL'S THEME]**.*)*

FANNY. Ariel, the magical sprite.

> *(**FANNY** creates the zip and zing of a creature streaking here and there.)*

(ARIEL). All hail, great master! I come to answer thy best pleasure; I boarded the king's ship and flamed amazement! The king's son, Ferdinand, with hair up-staring, – then like reeds, not hair – cried, "Hell is empty And all the devils are here!"

(PROSPERO). But are they, Ariel, safe?

(ARIEL). Not a hair perish'd; In troops I have dispersed them 'bout the isle.

(PROSPERO). Ariel, thy charge exactly is perform'd: but there's more work.

(ARIEL). More toil? Let me remember thee what thou hast promised. My liberty!

FANNY. *(Looking up from the book.)* There you are. *Liberté.* We shall meet this word again and again in the course of the play. Freedom. When I was sixteen years old…

> *(She looks at **THE PIANIST**.)*

No, no. He's right. I must be good.

> *(She goes back to the book. Is about to read, but stops. Coughs an obviously feigned cough.)*

Oh, dear.

> *(She crosses to the chair, where she sits and pours a glass of water. Leans forward and speaks to the audience as if taking them into her confidence.)*

The only time of my entire life I felt unequivocally free was that summer I returned home from Paris. I sang, wrote poetry, entertained the stream of visitors to our country cottage at Weybridge.

"Fanny Fair," that's what my father called me. And I – glancing occasionally into my glass… *(Peering into an imaginary mirror.)* could only agree.

I am Miranda. My features, delicately chiseled; my skin radiant and clear; my hair, black and shiny as printer's ink. My parents – Father especially – looked to the day when numerous young gentlemen would call at my door who were handsome, well-bred, and very, very... Yes!

(*Hurrying to the book.*)

Very much like this fellow here.

(**THE PIANIST** *plays the sinister* [**MUSIC 05 – CALIBAN INTERRUPTED**] *theme.*)

No, no!

(**THE PIANIST** *stops.*)

I'm skipping a few pages ahead. "Enter the King's son, Ferdinand?"

(**THE PIANIST** *all but growls as he turns ahead in his music. He then pounds out* [**MUSIC 05a – COME UNTO THESE YELLOW SANDS**]. **FANNY** *must shout to be heard above the music.*)

(**FERDINAND**). Sitting on a bank,
weeping again the king my father's wreck,
this music...

(*Shouting at* **THE PIANIST**.)

"CREPT"...BY ME UPON THE WATERS!

(**THE PIANIST** *lowers the volume.*)

FANNY. Prospero and Miranda enter. Prospero points to Ferdinand.

(**PROSPERO**). Say what thou seest yond.

(**MIRANDA**). (*Mouth dropping open.*) What is't? A spirit?

(PROSPERO). No, wench. This gallant was in the wreck;
and thou mightst call him a goodly person.

(MIRANDA). I might call him
a thing divine, for nothing natural
I ever saw so noble.

FANNY. Here Ferdinand discovers Miranda.

(FERDINAND). O you wonder! If you be maid or no?

(MIRANDA). No wonder, sir; But certainly a maid.

(FERDINAND). O, if a virgin,
and your affection not gone forth, I'll make you
the queen of Naples!

(PROSPERO). Soft, sir! Thou dost here usurp the name
thou owest not!

(MIRANDA). Beseech you, father!

(PROSPERO). Come.
I'll manacle thy neck and feet together:
Sea-water shalt thou drink; thy food shall be wither'd
roots and acorn husks!

FANNY. *(Sighing.)* Handsome boy, pretty girl, love at first
sight, a parent's hysterical objection. What adolescent
girl doesn't hunger for such a scene? I certainly did.
Unfortunately –

> **(THE PIANIST** *interrupts with a loud,
> discordant* **[MUSIC 05b – ANGRY CHORD]**.
> **FANNY** *charges over to him.)*

Is it not possible, given the finality of tonight's
performance, I MIGHT BE OF A MOOD TO
DIGRESS? What is it? Do you have a more important
engagement elsewhere this evening?!

> **(THE PIANIST** *sits there. Erect, unflinching.
> **FANNY** *recovers, turns to the audience.)*

Unfortunately...the first suitor to call at my door isn't a Ferdinand at all. It is a foul and malicious creature.

Steals into my room one night, kisses me on my cheek, and there appears on the spot...a tiny, red, blister. Then he kisses me again. And again and AGAIN! Until my face is a single, searing red flame! I wake up screaming,

(YOUNG FANNY). Mother!

FANNY. Seconds later she's in my room with a lantern. But the moment the light falls on my face she stumbles back. Stands there staring at me mute and paralyzed.

(YOUNG FANNY). Mummy! What's wrong with me?! MUMMY.

(MOTHER). Oh, my baby.

(YOUNG FANNY). What is it?! MUMMY!

FANNY. She can't bring herself to say the word. Smallpox. For weeks I am lost in delirium, more weeks in bed too exhausted to move. When at last I feel strong enough, all I want is my mirror.

(MOTHER). No, Fanny!

FANNY. But I pull myself across the room and step before the glass. Merciful God. I hardly recognize the image staring back. The skin on my face. It's thick and gouged, my features warped and blunted, even my hair hangs limp and dull as lead. I am suddenly plain. Beyond plain. I am hideous. Once the pretty, blushing Miranda, now...

(*To* **THE PIANIST.***)* Now enter Caliban...

> (**THE PIANIST** *goes back a few pages in the music.*)

...a loathsome, scaly-skinned monster,

> (**THE PIANIST** *plays* **[MUSIC 06 – CALIBAN]**.*)*

...who springs on Prospero and Miranda.

(CALIBAN). A south-west blow and blister you all o'er! This island's mine, by Sycorax my mother, which thou takest from me!

(PROSPERO). Thou most lying slave, I have used thee, Filth as thou art, with human care, till thou didst seek to violate the honour of my child.

(CALIBAN). O ho, O ho! Thou didst prevent me; I had peopled else this isle with Calibans.

(PROSPERO). I pitied thee, took pains to make thee speak.

(CALIBAN). You taught me language; and my profit on't

Is, I know how to curse. The red plague rid you

For learning me your language!

FANNY. *(Touching her face.)* The Red Plague. Certainly rid us of "Fanny Fair," did it not? Oh, I brooded for a time. I even tried my hand at cursing.

(YOUNG FANNY). Bloody pox!

FANNY. Finally, my mother – ever practical, ever candid...

(MOTHER). Fanny, it's time you considered a career. Let's face it, child, your prospects for marriage have clearly gone the way of your looks!

FANNY. But I have a career! Since childhood my one dream is to become a writer. And now I am. In the two years since Paris, I have penned poems, essays –

(Without thinking to **THE PIANIST**.*)*

– a complete five-act play!

(**THE PIANIST** *turns a page of his music...
A beat.)*

Yes, of course.

(Hurrying to the lectern.)

Act Two, Scene One. Another part of the island.

(*Looking up.*) Ariel, as he explained, has dispersed the shipwrecked survivors about the island. In one part, Prince Ferdinand has just lost his heart to Miranda. In another Trinculo and Stephano wander alone. In this scene, we find the Royal Party searching in vain for the King's son. As they do, old Gonzalo rhapsodizes on the glorious utopia he would create were he king of this island.

(GONZALO). No occupation; all men idle, all;

And women too, but innocent and pure;

All things in common nature should produce all foison, all abundance. I would with such perfection govern, sir, to excel the golden age.

FANNY. Golden age, indeed. My father! To his final breath, Charles Kemble held that one day Covent Garden would "excel" as Britain's Arcadia to the performing arts! Poor man. One afternoon – nineteen years old – I arrive home to find my mother in hysterics.

(MOTHER). Your father is being been sued! The walls of Covent Garden are plastered with notices of closure!

(YOUNG FANNY). Bloody Covent Garden!

(MOTHER). He was...wondering. Do you think you have any...talent for the stage?

FANNY. There! Try as I might to flee my heritage it snares me like a iron trap.

(YOUNG FANNY). But I'm too deformed to go on stage! Who will I play, Richard the Third?

(MOTHER). Your father wishes to test your voice at Covent Garden. Prepare something to recite. Prepare Juliet.

(YOUNG FANNY). Juliet? You cannot be serious!

FANNY. Oh, but she is.

FANNY. The very next morning Father escorts me to Covent Garden where I stand facing the vast empty amphitheatre. The darkened stage creaks like the deck of a ship. Above me the huge canvas drops hang like sails. I look out at the endless waves of chairs draped in gray cotton dust covers, and I am seized by the image of Miranda, trapped on that rotten boat, the angry sea pressing in from all sides...

(CHARLES). *(Calling from the auditorium.)* Fanny? We're waiting.

FANNY. *(Stepping forward.)* I speak my speech.

The very next afternoon the front page of *The London Times* proclaims in bold typeface:

"Charles Kemble announces the debut on Covent Garden's stage of his daughter, Fanny, in William Shakespeare's masterpiece, *Romeo and Juliet*. The play will open in...three...weeks...time!"

THREE WEEKS? Juliet! The most celebrated tragic ingénue of all time! Me! Who has never uttered a single line on stage in her life, forced to absorb an entire profession, memorize thousands of words, learn to move, to concert my movements with other actors, receive and deliver cues, all the while speaking complex metaphorical language IN IAMBIC PENTAMETERS! Three weeks!

As a kind of perverse moral support Mother is to accompany me as Lady Capulet. Father will play Mercutio. The part of Romeo is given to Mr. Abott, a man almost old as my father!

(Sitting.) The night of my debut I wait backstage attended by my dear Aunt Dall who patiently reapplies rouge to my cheeks as often as my terror-filled tears wash it off.

Mr. Keely – the old man playing Peter, the servant – comes over and pats my hand.

(**MR. KEELY**). Never you mind the audience, Miss Kemble. Jus' think of them as...as so many rows of cabbages!

FANNY. *(Looking at the book.)* Then I hear Lady Capulet call from the stage.

> (**FANNY** *glances at* **THE PIANIST**. *Looks back to the book. Finally turning to* **THE PIANIST**.*)*

I loathe asking you this, but you will excuse me, won't you, if I take a slight detour into another play?

> *(As* **FANNY** *gets up and starts for the lectern,* **THE PIANIST** *stands, bows curtly to the audience, even more curtly to* **FANNY**, *then walks off.* **FANNY** *can't believe it. She starts after him.)*

What are you...

> *(Stopping at the screen looking off.)*

Well, I... FINE THEN!

> *(She turns to the book and searches for the place.)*

Romeo And Juliet, Act One, Scene Three. A room in Capulet's house. Enter Lady Capulet and Nurse.

> *(She reads.)*

(**LADY CAPULET**). Nurse! Where's my daughter? Call her forth to me!

(**NURSE**). Now, by my maidenhead, at twelve year old,
I bade her come. What, lamb! What, ladybird!
God forbid! Where's this girl? What, Juliet!
JULIET, I SAY!

FANNY. I stand in the wings. No power on earth will pry me from this spot. Just then my Aunt Dall gives an emphatic push! I shoot across the stage straight into the arms of my mother, and forthwith attach myself to her like some fifth limb.

(LADY CAPULET). Nurse, give leave awhile, we must talk in secret.

> (**LADY CAPULET** *tries to free herself of* **JULIET**. *But doesn't succeed.*)

Nurse, come back again!

Thou know'st my daughter's of a pretty age.

(NURSE). Faith, I can tell her age unto an hour.

(LADY CAPULET). She's not fourteen.

(NURSE). I'll lay fourteen of my teeth

– And yet, to my teeth be it spoken, I have but four –
She is not fourteen.

FANNY. Mother yanks herself free as Nurse rambles on...

(NURSE). Thou wilt fall backward when thou comest to age; Wilt thou not, Jule? It "stinted" and said "Ay."

FANNY. There is a sudden and deathly silence. Nurse repeats the line.

(NURSE). It "stinted" and said "Ay"?

FANNY. The next speech is mine! What are the words? Stint. Stint!

(JULIET). *(In a near-whisper.)* And stint thou too! I pray thee, nurse, say I.

FANNY. As Nurse and Mother continue the scene, I can sense the audience looking at them, not me. I lift my eyes. And there in the lantern-light reflecting off the scenery, the faces of the spectators glow softly. And... they do resemble "so many rows of cabbages!"

(LADY CAPULET). Speak briefly, can you like of Paris' love?

FANNY. Good God. Every "cabbage" in the hall now turns to me. But in their faces – they are not repulsed by my ugliness. In fact they seem eager to hear what I had to say.

(JULIET). I'll look to like if looking liking move...

(She turns to the audience.)

but no more deep will I endart mine eye

than your consent gives strength to make it fly.

(LADY CAPULET). Juliet, the county stays!

(NURSE). Go, girl, seek happy nights to happy days!

FANNY. Happy days, indeed! In the next scene, the ballroom with its music and masks, I begin to forget myself. By the following scene, on the balcony, for all I know, I have become Juliet. Like it or not, the blood of Mrs. Siddons flows through my veins, too. From here on, I do not return into myself until all is over, and what follows is a tumultuous storm of applause, congratulations, tears, embraces, and a general explosion of relief.

It would be difficult to imagine anything more radical than the change one evening could make in every aspect of my life. From an insignificant, ugly schoolgirl, I am suddenly the toast of London, a little lion of society. Sir Thomas Lawrence, painter to the King, arrives with brushes and easel. I sit...

(Sitting on the now vacant piano bench and posing.) ... for weeks...

(Holding the pose.) When I finally gaze at the finished portrait... Saints be praised, Lawrence is truly Godlike! What does Isaiah say?

"The crooked shall be made straight and the rough made smooth"? Voila! The reincarnation of Fanny Fair!

FANNY. My portrait is immediately reproduced and soon all about London my countenance is staring up at me. From plates, saucers, serving trays, jewelry boxes, scarves, handkerchiefs. Throughout the city ladies' hairdos suddenly take on the "Kemble Curl." From the stage each night I look into the pit where scores of young men sport my likeness painted on their neckties! My every word, mood, gesture is recorded in the daily newspapers. But why? Are people blind? I am not Miranda! Look at me! I am Caliban! The creature in this play.

(**FANNY** *stops. Looks at the book.*)

The play! Dear Lord.

(*Hurrying to the lectern.*) You pay good money to hear a reading of *The Tempest*, and instead I bombard you with...

(*Flipping back in the book.*) Where are we? Oh, yes. Sebastian and Antonio are plotting to kill the King...

(*Thinking about it a moment.*) Let's skip that.

(*Turning a page.*) Ah. Enter Caliban hauling logs.

(CALIBAN). All the infections that the sun sucks up on Prosper Fall and make him by inch-meal a disease!

FANNY. This is Act Two, Scene Two, by the way.

(CALIBAN). Lo, now, lo!
Here comes a spirit of his, and to torment me
for bringing wood in slowly. I'll fall flat;
perchance he will not mind me.

FANNY. Enter Trinculo, the King's jester.

(**FANNY** *provides thunder and lightning.*)

(TRINCULO). Here's neither bush nor shrub, and another storm brewing; what have we here? A man or a fish?

Smells like a fish.

(*More thunder.*)

My best way is to creep under his gabardine;
misery acquaints a man with strange bedfellows.

FANNY. Enter Stephano, the butler singing a...

> (**FANNY** *stops. Looks at the unmanned piano. Resolutely she marches offstage. Finally, some distance into the wings.*)

(*Offstage.*) Do you intend to leave me stranded out here all evening? Very well, I apologize! Yes, yes, I promise.

> (*Entering the stage followed by a pouting* **PIANIST.**)

We will forge through *The Tempest* sans l'interruption!

(*To the audience as she crosses back center.*) This, above all, is why I wish to retire!

(*Reading.*) Stephano, the butler, carrying a large jug of wine.

> (**THE PIANIST** *plays* [MUSIC 07 – STEPHANO'S JIG].)

(**STEPHANO**). (*Singing.*)
FOR SHE HAD A TONGUE WITH A TANG,
WOULD CRY TO A SAILOR, "GO HANG!"
SHE LOVED NOT THE SAVOUR OF TAR NOR OF PITCH,
YET A TAILOR MIGHT SCRATCH HER
WHERE'ER SHE DID ITCH:
THEN TO SEA, BOYS, AND LET HER GO HANG!

> (*He drinks.*)

(**CALIBAN**). (*Sitting up.*) Do not torment me, prithee;
I'll bring my wood home faster!

(STEPHANO). Have we devils here? This is some monster of the isle...WITH FOUR LEGS! who hath got, as I take it, an ague. Come on, open your mouth; here is that which will give language to you.

> (**STEPHANO** *pours the liquor down* **CALIBAN**'s *gullet.*)

(CALIBAN). *(Instantly intoxicated.)* That's a brave god and bears celestial liquor.

I will kneel to him.

[MUSIC 07a – THE BANJO]

(Singing drunkenly.)

'BAN, 'BAN, C'CALIBAN
HAS A NEW MASTER: GET A NEW MAN.
FREEDOM, HEY-DAY! HEY-DAY!
FREEDOM, HEY-DAY! HEY-DAY!

FANNY. "Freedom." There we are again!

I performed the star-crossed lover upward of one hundred and twenty times with Covent Garden filled to overflowing every night. My debut does liberate me to a degree. I now have money. New frocks. A horse of my very own. Unfortunately, the moment my attraction as Juliet wanes, I'm cast in a muddy lament. *The Fatal Marriage...*

For more than a century, British theatre was obsessed with fatality. As witnessed by the titles of its plays. *The Fatal Contract, Fatal Discovery, Fatal Extravagance, Fatal Friendship, Fatal Jealousy, The Fatal Kiss, Fatal Letter*, and so on down an entire alphabet of woe.

It's no wonder one critic referred to this era as the "winter solstice" of English Drama.

Is there, you may well ask, some small respite for me at season's close? Not in the least. Off we go each summer touring the provinces: Manchester to Edinburgh,

Glasgow to Dublin. My efforts do greatly enhance Covent Garden's coffers, but the amount is insufficient to forestall the inevitable. In our third season father learns that his theatre is bankrupt and will soon close. I repress a scream of joy. Thrilled that I can, at last, cast off this repugnant profession; return once more to my writing.

Until Father rushes in waving a fat contract.

(CHARLES). Fanny, our prayers have been answered. We are invited to spend the next two years touring the principal theatres of America!

    *(***YOUNG FANNY*** screams.)*

(YOUNG FANNY). Need I remind you that the United States is populated with outlaws! And the only country in the civilized world still supporting slavery!

(CHARLES). But other British actors have made the trip, Kean, Macready. And returned far wealthier for their pains!

(YOUNG FANNY). Then you go. By yourself!

(CHARLES). They don't want me by myself. All I'm asking is to earn enough so your mother and I can retire to the South of France where living costs are moderate. Can you deny us that?

FANNY. On August first, 1832, Father and I – along with dear Aunt Dall, as chaperone – arrive on the dock in Liverpool with twenty-one trunks filled mostly with stage costumes.

(Standing next to the piano.) Nowadays, a modern steamship crosses the three thousand miles of Atlantic in ten days. Our voyage took a full five weeks. Five! With me... *(Clutching the edge of the piano.)* ...hanging over the rail bawling Gonzalo's lament, "I would fain die a dry..."

> *(She realizes that she's staring directly into the face of* **THE PIANIST**.*)*

FANNY. Oh! I've done it again! Wandered off. Go ahead. You may leave! And you do so... *(A little curtsy.)* with my blessing.

> *(***THE PIANIST** *stands and starts off.* **FANNY** *taps a note on the piano and hums as she returns to the lectern.* **THE PIANIST** *stops. Vexed at the thought that he's not indispensable.)*

Act Three, Scene One.

> *(***THE PIANIST** *goes back to the piano.)*

Poor, desolate Miranda finds her sweet Ferdinand laboring like a beast of burden.

> *(***THE PIANIST** *plays* [MUSIC 08 – THE RELUCTANT YELLOW SANDS]. **FANNY** *turns to him.)*

What? Still here?

> *(***THE PIANIST** *rolls his eyes in frustration but continues.* **FANNY** *– with a look of quiet triumph – reads to* **THE PIANIST**.*)*

(MIRANDA). Alas, if you'll sit down, I'll bear your logs the while.

(FERDINAND). No, precious creature! But I do beseech you – Chiefly that I might set it in my prayers – What is your name?

(MIRANDA). Miranda.

(FERDINAND). Admired Miranda! The very instant that I saw you, did my heart fly to your service; there resides To make me slave to it!

FANNY. He vows to be her slave. How touching. How telling.

(Sitting. Sipping her water.) Following our engagement in New York City, we move on to Philadelphia. One morning I come down to find a pretty spoken youth sitting with Father, a Mr. Pierce Butler.

(BUTLER). I have read in the newspapers that you are not only a celebrated actress but a devoted horsewoman as well. Would you do me the honor of one day riding with me?

FANNY. What a pleasant surprise. For most women, the way to her heart is through jewels and finery. For me it is atop a sweating horse.

From then on – the entire tour – young Mr. Butler is our constant companion. Though reluctant to discuss his personal life, I do piece together that he is very well-bred. Aristocratic, rich, cavalier. Very much a young Ferdinand; and very much devoted to me.

I realize, of course, it's my fame that lures him. Believe me, I know how I look. In fact among the few newspaper clippings I've saved is one quoting a West Point cadet by the name of Robert E. Lee who was heard to say:

(ROBERT E. LEE). *(Southern accent.)* On stage Miss Kemble is the most beautiful of women. But up close – I declare, the lady is next door to homely.

FANNY. Again the illusion of theatre. Miranda by stage light; but in the cold, gray dawn of day...

        (THE PIANIST *plays* **[MUSIC 09 – CALIBAN – ILLUSION OF THEATRE].***)*

Indeed!

        (She returns to the book.)

Act Three, Scene Two...

FANNY. *(At the book.)* Here we find Caliban and Stephano conspiring to murder Prospero.

(CALIBAN). My noble lord. 'Tis a custom with Prosper,
I' th' afternoon to sleep: there thou mayst brain him!

(STEPHANO). Monster, I will kill this man: his daughter
and I will be king and queen – save our graces!

[MUSIC 09a – THE FLOUT 'EM AND SCOUT 'EM WALTZ]

(Singing.)

FLOUT 'EM AND SCOUT 'EM
AND SCOUT 'EM AND FLOUT 'EM.
THOUGHT IS FREE!

FANNY. Much like this rowdy scene our repertoire in the United States consisted of comedies. Actually, we performed tragedies, mostly, but they came out comedies. Due quite frankly to the so-called actors with whom I was forced to share the stage. Worst were the Romeos.

In Baltimore I played opposite one fellow who, in the final moments of the play – the famous graveyard scene – swallows his poison like a good boy and dies. I kneel by his side prepared to follow.

"Oh, happy dagger!" I exclaim reaching for the much needed instrument. "Sir," I finally say, sotto voce, "where the devil is your dagger?" He looks up at me and non sotto voce...

(BALTIMORE ROMEO). 'Pon my word, Ma'am, Don't rightly know.

FANNY. *(Standing, again with difficulty.)* I'm here to report that Juliet did not stab herself to death that night. She died, poor thing, of heart failure!

To preserve my sanity, I steal away and record my notions of America on paper. Not only the noisy celebrities who constantly court us, but the country's quiet face as well. The chambermaids, livery men, the American Negro, this dark anomaly here in the land of "liberty and justice for all."

Near the end of the tour a Philadelphia firm actually offers to publish my random sketches and even presents me with a cash advance! Here is cold, hard proof that I can return home and earn my livelihood in a profession that I enjoy!

But then – oh dear God – my Aunt Dall is killed in a carriage accident. This dear lady. More parent to me these last years than my own father.

My Father! Word arrives from London that Covent Garden is once again fiscally afloat and we are invited back! Father as General Manager, me as prima donna!

(YOUNG FANNY). *(Stamping her foot.)* No! I have paid my bond. The tour has earned you a fortune!

FANNY. Here I learn that due to bad investments, Father is all but destitute.

(Looking to heaven.) "Dear God, shall I be forced to live my entire life in front of an audience?"

(To the audience.) You can clearly see God's answer.

    (THE PIANIST *plays the Ferdinand Theme:* **[MUSIC 10 – GOD'S ANSWER: PROSPERO].***)*

Yes.

(Going to the book.) *The Tempest* now takes a major turn as Prospero...

    (Looking out at the audience, she stops.)

Oh, dear. The perplexed look on your faces... Is anyone having difficulty following the story of *The Tempest*? Don't be modest, raise your hands.

FANNY. Oh, *mon Dieu*! I forget that in America William Shakespeare's plays are not the mother's milk they are in Britain. *The Tempest,* though long in substance is short in plot. It's quite simple. Really.

(Illustrating.) Here is Prospero, Duke of Milan; over here an enchanted island home to Ariel and Caliban. Back in Milan, Prospero's throne is usurped by his brother and the King of Naples. Prospero, set adrift with his daughter, arrives here on the island and learns sorcery. Twelve years later, his Italian enemies chance by. Prospero raises a storm, sinks their ship, and spends the next three hours tormenting his hapless victims! Which is where we are now. Questions? Excellent.

(At the book.) Prospero takes pity on Ferdinand.

[MUSIC 10a – PROSPERO AND FERDINAND]

(PROSPERO). If I have too austerely punish'd you,

Your compensation makes amends.

Take my daughter. She is thine own.

FANNY. Father and I conclude our American tour here in Philadelphia. As we gather our belongings and prepare to sail for home, Pierce Butler arrives and urges me to stay.

(YOUNG FANNY). Are you asking me to abandon my parents?

(BUTLER). I am asking you to marry me.

(YOUNG FANNY). Marry you? You cannot be serious!

FANNY. But he is! Pledges like young Ferdinand to be my slave! Offers me a gracious, carefree, and – at last – a respectable life. I hurry to tell Father.

(CHARLES). Fanny. How can you be so heartless? A season or two more. Think of your mother!

FANNY. I do think of my mother. Living her entire life under the pall of poverty. And so, to Father I give every penny I've earned on our two-year tour, thirty-five thousand gold American dollars. To Pierce Butler…I give my hand.

*(***THE PIANIST*** plays a few bars of Mendelssohn's* **[MUSIC 11 – WEDDING MARCH]. FANNY** *smiles at him, turns to the book.)*

Prospero now summons a pageant of deities to celebrate the forthcoming union of Ferdinand and Miranda. Juno, Goddess of Marriage, blesses the couple.

[MUSIC 11a – HONOUR, RICHES, MARRIAGE-BLESSING]

(JUNO). Honour, riches, marriage-blessing,
Long continuance, and increasing.

FANNY. Pierce's and my wedding is a cause célèbre! Following which Father... *(Waving goodbye.)* ...sails, at last, for home.

Those first few months alone Pierce and I are Ferdinand and Miranda. Upon whom Juno's blessings are quick to bear fruit. Soon, I am not only wife, but by spring I'll be mother as well.

That fall – the renovations to our house not yet complete – we take temporary refuge with Pierce's brother, John, and his wife, Gabriella, in their elegant home on Chestnut Street. One evening the men are in the drawing room discussing some difficulty down in... "Georgia." When I ask the nature of the problem Pierce dismisses me.

(BUTLER). It's business and none of your concern.

FANNY. Oh, really. I quickly locate Gabriella at her needlework and say offhandedly,

(YOUNG FANNY). The men are in the other room smoking cigars and fussing over that...trouble down in Georgia.

(GABRIELLA). Oh yes, the new overseer.

(YOUNG FANNY). Overseer? Of what?

(GABRIELLA). Why the plantations, of course.

FANNY. As the woman prattles on I learn that on island farms off the coast of Georgia there dwell more than eight hundred people who, like the barns and mules, wagons and plows, are listed as Butler family assets. Eight hundred people whose labor permits us to enjoy a life of unbounded luxury and leisure. Eight hundred men, women, and children, who are, in short, Mr. Butler's, and now my...slaves.

(YOUNG FANNY). SLAVES?

(GABRIELLA). Certainly you know about Sea Island plantations, Fanny. Heavens. Don't tell me you're prejudiced against slavery!

(YOUNG FANNY). Madam, I am an Englishwoman. In whom the absence of such prejudice would be disgraceful!

FANNY. In the months that follow I learn that my husband is not only one of the largest slave holders in North America, he suddenly considers himself the patriarch of his new family and demands that I submit my will utterly to his!

Who is this person? Where is my beloved Ferdinand? The image of Miranda trapped aboard that foundering ship appears before my eyes. No, no! I push it away. If Pierce Butler thinks I will dutifully "step back..."

I had never considered involving myself in the debate over American slavery, but now my mind is ablaze with moral indignation!

Oh, dear Lord. Just as I have begun to believe the curtain has fallen on my life as a public pageant, here I am, center stage; cast in an even more outrageous folly:

Fanny Kemble, The Fatal Abolitionist!

> (**FANNY** *turns away, pauses to collect herself.*
> *She goes to the small table and pours herself*
> *a glass of water.* **THE PIANIST** *gently plays*

[MUSIC 12 – END OF "MIDSUMMER NIGHT'S DREAM"].*)*

Our revels now are ended. These our actors were all spirits and are melted into air, into thin air:

*(**FANNY** turns to the book.)*

(PROSPERO). And, like the baseless fabric of this vision,

The cloud-capped towers, the gorgeous palaces,

The solemn temples –

FANNY. *(Looking up.)* Yes, yes, I can hear your thoughts! "How could she have married the man without knowing the source of his enormous wealth? My answer? "I did not know because Mr. Butler did not tell me." And that is true. Or... The very nature of deception requires – does it not? – at least some participation by the victim. We believe quite often what we want to believe. And at that time, I very much wanted to – needed to – believe that Pierce Butler was my refuge, my liberator. "Liberté."

"We are such stuff as dreams are made on."

(Reading.) The Tempest, Act Three, Scene Three. Enter the Royal party still in search of Ferdinand.

(GONZALO). By'r lakin, I can go no further, sir;

By your patience, I needs must rest me.

(ALONZO). Old lord, I cannot blame thee,

(THE PIANIST *plays* **[MUSIC 13 – WHAT HARMONY/HARPY].***)*

What harmony is this? My good friends, hark!

FANNY. Prospero reveals a table laid with a sumptuous feast. But before they can take a bite, Ariel enters, in the form of a harpy.

(The piano thunders.)

(ARIEL). *(Screeching like a predatory bird.)* You are three men of sin, whom Destiny

Hath caused to belch up you here on this island

But remember that you three from Milan

did supplant good Prospero…

FANNY. "…exposed unto the sea him and his innocent child."

(To the audience.) One autumn – two years after our marriage – my husband allows me to visit my parents while he's off to Georgia and his plantations. With my infant daughter, Sarah, we set sail, and almost immediately our ship is caught in a savage whirlwind that assaults us for four solid days. At the height of the storm, the frightful uproar of the elements, the delirious plunging and rearing of the convulsed ship becomes so intense I'm convinced that we are doomed. My terror slowly surrenders to exhaustion, exhaustion to submission. Finally, to soothe my infant daughter I sing…my last feeble defense against the unbridled fury of the storm.

Think of Prospero cast adrift aboard that rudderless ship clinging to his child. Once a "Prince of Power" now a creature with no more control over his fate than a feather in a whirlwind. Absolute powerlessness. Imagine the effect it has. If it does not destroy, then most certainly it must transform.

    (Reading:)

(PROSPERO). My high charms work and these mine enemies are all knit up in their distractions; they now are in my power!

FANNY. Power! The arch enemy of Liberté. Here are the guts of *The Tempest*. Nearly every scene pits those possessing power against those who do not. One does not appreciate power, does she, until she has it completely stripped away.

My American Journal. This was our first clash of wills. As I am preparing the manuscript for publication – this record of my journey to America – I feel justified in expressing my viewpoint on the issue of slavery. Pierce flies into a rage!

(BUTLER). I forbid you to publish one word!

(YOUNG FANNY). You forbid me? On whose authority?

(BUTLER). I am Master of this house!

(YOUNG FANNY). I am Mistress of myself!

(BUTLER). You made a vow to love, honor and obey me!

(YOUNG FANNY). That was...an ecclesiastical formality!

FANNY. Not so! Not to Pierce, who believed, solely by virtue of his sex, that he was my superior and thereby commanded my absolute obedience! It matters not that my journal – though admittedly controversial – proves to be an enormous success. The man is unyielding.

His behavior becomes so oppressive, one night I pack a bag and depart to find a hotel until I can arrange passage home to England. But hotels, transport on ships...these cost money. And I, having given my entire fortune to my father, am, for the first time, penniless.

There is a look of quiet triumph on Pierce's face when I – bag in hand – return home. What happens? Only moments before we were Ferdinand and Miranda. Now. Prospero and Caliban.

(Returning to the book.) Here. Listen to Prospero:

(PROSPERO). Caliban, a born devil, on whose nature

nurture can never stick; on whom my pains,

humanely taken, all, all lost, quite lost.

FANNY. Pierce often described his slaves this way, as creatures "on whose nature nurture could never stick." And held, as did most of his peers, that the Negro was less than human and could not learn.

FANNY. "If they cannot learn," I'd ask, "why are there laws against teaching them?" As there are laws against slaves owning property, their attending church; against miscegenation. This last was my favorite. It was illegal for a white man to marry a black woman, but perfectly lawful for him to make her the mother of his children.

It was my husband's practice to visit his plantations each winter when the threat of yellow fever had subsided. In the fall of 1838, as he makes plans to depart, I press him to take me along. For years Pierce has affirmed that he is a humane master, the overseer is kind, the Negroes remarkably well cared for. But I wish to see this "human property" of mine for myself.

(BUTLER). But there is no accommodation for a woman.

(YOUNG FANNY). I don't care. I was an actress. I am accustomed to living in hovels.

FANNY. Finally – more from exasperation than good judgment – he agrees. We depart for Georgia on December twenty-first – Pierce and I with Sarah, now three years old, and little Fan at seven months. We arrive a week later aboard a flat bottom barge from which, like Prospero and Miranda, we disembark on "our" tropic isle. Saint Simon, Georgia. We are greeted – not by a curious Caliban – but by a vociferous multitude that all but lift us into the air!

I decide from the onset to keep a journal, and my first entries describe the pitiful conditions in which the slaves exist. But it's not until I discover the large, two-story hospital, that I see the true nature of this enterprise.

The first floor houses the Women's Quarters. I enter and – oh dear God – scores of creatures lie prostrate on the dirt floor, without bed, mattress, blanket; some in the agony of childbirth, others have just delivered, still more are groaning in the anguish of miscarriage.

Here lie some burning with fever, here some chilled with cold, most aching with rheumatism. The drafts and dampness, the dirt, noise, stench, fleas, flies, rodents make their already grave suffering all but unbearable. I stand in the midst of them perfectly unable to speak, tears pouring from my eyes. But when I reach for some kindling to make a fire, there is a universal cry of horror!

(FEMALE SLAVE). MISSIS! What for you lift wood? Got plenty of us to do it!

FANNY. Pray note, here is the hospital of an estate where the owner is humane, the overseer kind, and the Negroes remarkably well cared for. I leave this "refuge" hours later my clothes covered with filth and filled with vermin and go straight to vent my indignation on Mr. Butler.

(BUTLER). Now Fanny. That's the way it's always been.

FANNY. On this island – owned, governed and regulated by men – I am perhaps the first to attend to the "female" slave. I become their instant patron. Every day troops of them arrive with simple requests – a morsel of mutton, scrap of flannel, piece of soap – most on behalf of their children. I am a nursing mother myself, how can I not hearken to their needs? One evening a gang of pregnant women – pregnant, mind you – beseech me to beg "Massa" to reduce their workload in the fields. I lead the procession to my husband who stands there – soft and white as fresh bread with the crust removed.

(BUTLER). Liars. They are incurable liars!

(YOUNG FANNY). Liars? Their festering sores, bent and broken bones, gaunt, skeletal children. These are lies?

(BUTLER). *(Stamping his foot.)* Enough!

FANNY. And I suddenly realize that whatever respect I once held for this man is gone. This island is a mirror of Gonzalo's Utopia, isn't it? Not for the slaves, but for the white "Massas" and their families.

(She turns to the book.)

(GONZALO). No occupation; all men idle, all;
And women too, but innocent and pure...

FANNY. All things in common nature should produce,
Without sweat or endeavour, all foison, all abundance...
When I can stand it no longer I tell Pierce:

(YOUNG FANNY). If you will not permit me to help these people I can no longer continue to live here among them.

(BUTLER). You have no choice, now do you?

FANNY. And there it is. Mr. Butler does not own eight hundred slaves. He owns eight hundred and one.

> *(Picking up her glass of water, she crosses towards the piano.)*

Ironically, it is the slaves themselves who maintain my spirits. Like the strapping young men rowing up and down the river chanting whimsical rhymes.

(To **THE PIANIST**.*)* My favorite is one that must have washed down from up north.

[MUSIC 14 – BOATMAN'S DANCE]

(Singing.)

HI! O! THE BOATMAN ROW

> **(THE PIANIST** *quickly picks up the tune.)*

GOING DOWN THE RIVER ON THE O-HI-O.

(To the audience.) The island's beauty and wonder. This, too, surprises me afresh every hour. Flowers in bloom year round; grey mosses hanging from outstretched oaks like disheveled hair. The jubilee of mockingbirds nesting in the varnished evergreens. And at night...

(Looking at the book.) Of course. Listen to Caliban:

> *(She goes to the book.)*

(CALIBAN). Be not afeard; the isle is full of noises,

(**THE PIANIST** *underscores with Mendelssohn:* [**MUSIC 15 – SOUNDS AND SWEET AIRS**].)

Sounds and sweet airs, that give delight and hurt not.

Sometimes a thousand twangling instruments

Will hum about mine ears, and sometime voices

That, if I then had waked after long sleep,

Will make me sleep again.

FANNY. Often at night as I sit at my desk transcribing my thoughts, the door opens stealthily, and one after another, black men and women troop in. They betake themselves to the hearth where they squat in a circle, the bright blaze from the huge pine logs shining on their sooty limbs and faces. They look like a ring of ebony idols perfectly absorbed in contemplating me.

My evening dress excites them no less than my continuous writing, for which they often express compassion, as if it must be more laborious than hoeing weeds.

(YOUNG FANNY). Well, what do you want?"

FANNY. Each figure springs up as if moved by machinery.

(OLD MAN). Just come say "ha do," Missis.

FANNY. And they troop out as noiselessly as they entered, into the night, like a procession of sable dreams.

My last weeks on the plantation I throw discretion to the wind. Against all rules, I pay a group of older boys hard cash to clear paths for me through the woods. I hold clandestine religious services. Read from the Bible, dwelling on the Book of "Exodus"!

I even go so far as to violate Georgia state law and teach a young slave named Aleck to read! I give him language. Good heavens, if Mr. Butler had found out he would have...

> (**THE PIANIST**, *caught up in her story, plays a hunting theme,* [**MUSIC 16 – HORN CALL/ UNREST**]. **FANNY** *turns to him.*)

FANNY. Yes! How Prospero dealt with Caliban's cut-throats! Release the dogs!

> (**FANNY** *barks, growls, snaps. Then suddenly bangs on the book.* **THE PIANIST** *stops playing.*)

How I wished for a pack of dogs that morning I found those two letters. Those two scheming, duplicitous letters!

> (**THE PIANIST** *is shocked. She turns to him.*)

Yes! Upon our return to Philadelphia.

(To the audience.) When I confront Pierce with the evidence rather than admit his infidelity, he berates me for invading his private papers!

What to do? Accept it?

> (**THE PIANIST** *frowns.*)

I should say not.

(To the audience.) Divorce is an option, at least here in Pennsylvania. But the children. Above all I must think of them. So I ask Pierce for a separation, one with unrestricted access to my daughters. He agrees on condition that I not return to the stage, promote the abolition cause, or publish anything without his approval.

Of course I don't realize when I move out that I am now a "femme couverte." "A married woman" with no legal rights other than through her husband. Everything I possess belongs to Pierce. Money I earn belongs to Pierce. Even the children belong to Pierce and no law compels him to let me even see them.

Thus for nearly two years I literally chase my girls about the country. That summer Pierce whisks them off to Rhode Island. In the fall he deposits them at the Butler farm. Even when they return to the city, I am permitted almost no contact. One time I meet them on the street walking with their governess, and they actually pass me without speaking. I run after.

(YOUNG FANNY). Sarah, how can you do this to your own mother?

(SARAH). Our governess told us not to speak to you. And father said, always obey your governess.

FANNY. As they walk away I stand there absolutely powerless to stop them. Absolute powerlessness. Now where have we heard that before?

No, no! I must shake off this groveling persona, find the funds to hire lawyers and recapture custody of my girls. The only source of such revenue open to me is, of course, the stage. Not in America, heaven forfend!

(THE PIANIST *plays* **[MUSIC 16a – RULE BRITANNIA]. FANNY** *bows to him.)*

I sail for home. Home. Where my father and a harvest of well-wishers welcome me. William Thackeray, my friend since adolescence, has just published his novel, *Vanity Fair*, and it's a huge success. I am not surprised. I have always possessed an instinct for people whose greatness is yet undiscovered – for cygnets rather than swans. Mendelssohn, Longfellow, Edward Fitzgerald. And a new young friend for whom I have huge expectations. The American, Henry James.

I know. I am in England to work, not to socialize.

My father, bless him, has received numerous offers for me to perform in London, but as I am now the ancient age of thirty-seven, I decide to try myself out in Manchester first. Although I experience less stage fright, I do notice more frequent lapses of attention. One night I almost miss my entrance in the third act of *School for Scandal*, and as I rush out on stage I completely forget the tune Lady Teazle should be humming. Whereupon I astonish both the audience and myself with:

(THE PIANIST *launches into* **[MUSIC 16b – BOATMAN DANCE 2]. FANNY** *smiles.)*

FANNY. Our penitent Pianist reads my mind.

(Singing with the piano.)

GOING DOWN THE RIVER ON THE O...HI...O!

(FANNY *laughs.* **THE PIANIST** *almost smiles.)*

When I do move on to London word awaits me from William Charles Macready, England's current leading actor. The gentleman wants us to perform together in a series of Shakespeare plays. Macready does have a reputation for abusing his fellow actors on stage, but the money he is offering...

Macready, you see, was an early proponent of a style now sweeping through the arts. It's called, "realism." Now I ask you, why would anyone crave "realism" in the Theatre? There is quite enough, thank you, right outside the front door! Like the afternoon a solicitor appears at "my" front door with that summons.

(Reading the imaginary document.) "You are hereby ordered to appear at the Honorable Court of Common Pleas, Philadelphia, Pennsylvania, to answer the charge filed by Pierce M. Butler for willful, malicious, and unwarranted desertion."

DESERTION?

"The Complainant seeks divorce *a vinculo matrimonii* and absolute custody of the couple's minor children: Sarah and Frances Anne."

Dear God in heaven, will this man's persecution of me never cease?

Macready and I close our Shakespeare series with a production of *Othello*. In the last act, the "execution scene"...

(To **THE PIANIST**.*)* Would you mind terribly if I...took a tiny peek into one more play?

> (**THE PIANIST** *quickly obliges by playing something dark,* [**MUSIC 17 – O, MA CHARMANTE, EPARGNEZ MOI!**].*)*

That's lovely.

(Hurrying to the book.) As the scene opens, I – as Desdemona – lie in bed asleep. Macready enters as Othello.

(**OTHELLO**). I'll not shed her blood nor scar that whiter skin of hers than snow...

FANNY. As he speaks I open my eyes slightly and, looking at him, I'm suddenly seized with the image of my husband.

(**OTHELLO**). Thou cunning'st pattern of excelling nature...

FANNY. A man who duped me into marrying him, reduced me to a possession, a trophy to display with his other conquests!

(**OTHELLO**). Have you pray'd tonight, Desdemona?

(**DESDEMONA**). Ay, my lord.

(**OTHELLO**). I would not kill thy unprepared spirit.

(**DESDEMONA**). Talk you of killing?

(**OTHELLO**). Ay, I do. Think on thy sins.

FANNY. *(Slamming her hand on the book.)* MY SINS! I feel the fury rise! How many Desdemonas have we seen acquiesce with wonderful equanimity to their assassination! Well, by Our Lady, that will not happen to this one!

(OTHELLO). Peace, and be still!

(DESDEMONA). No, by my life and soul!

FANNY. Macready is befuddled at first, but then...

(OTHELLO). Sweet soul, take heed, thou art on thy deathbed!

(DESDEMONA). Ay, but not yet to die!

FANNY. Macready comes at me clutching that soft white pillow...

(OTHELLO). Out, strumpet!

FANNY. But as he lunges at me, I throw my arms around his neck and hold on for dear life!

(OTHELLO). *(Trying to shake her off.)* Down, strumpet!

(DESDEMONA). Kill me tomorrow: let me live tonight!

FANNY. He wrenches back and forth unable to shake me off!

(OTHELLO). Nay, if you strive –

(DESDEMONA). But half an hour!

(OTHELLO). There is no pause!

(DESDEMONA). While I say one prayer!

(OTHELLO). IT IS TOO LATE!!

Macready suddenly yanks the bed curtains closed and then rips my arms from his neck and violently pushes me back on the bed. From the low growl escaping his throat I'm certain the man will, indeed, murder me. But the cries of an awaiting Emilia return him to the conclusion of the play.

I am panting. My arms and chest throb with pain. Tears pour from my eyes. But it is finally over. And here is one Desdemona who escaped being choked to death by her oppressive husband. One woman whose principles, pride, devotion to her children is not smothered by that soft white pillow of unbridled superiority!

Divorce me? DIVORCE ME?

We will see who divorces whom!

(**FANNY** *sits. Pours herself some water.*)

Oh my, I suspect you are wondering what on earth has happened to *The Tempest*. Poor little play.

In the fall of 1848, I sail back to America and submit my sixty-page response to Pierce Butler's charge. The text is promptly published word-for-word in the city's newspapers, and quite suddenly, my once self-assured husband becomes conciliatory. Would I agree to a compromise?

My lawyers urge me to refuse.

They yearn for my appearance before a jury of twelve good men and true, convinced that my "fatal" performance will melt even hearts of Pennsylvania limestone. My first impulse is to drag the suit to trial and feed every last morsel to the ravenous public. But my daughters. They already blame me for all this trouble. What satisfaction is there in winning only to lose them forever?

I therefore withdraw my opposition. And on November twenty-second, 1849, Butler wins his divorce. And yes, retains custody of our girls. I am awarded a two-month visitation each summer as well as a modest sum for support.

At least – praise God – I am emancipated. Liberté! My first act of which is to restore my maiden name. I do, however, retain one small relic of my marriage: the title, "Mrs." Mrs. Kemble.

(**FANNY** *sits there lost in thought.* **THE PIANIST** *leads her back with* [**MUSIC 18 – WHERE THE BEE SUCKS**]. **FANNY** *smiles.*)

FANNY. *(Singing softly.)*
MERRILY, MERRILY SHALL I LIVE NOW
UNDER THE BLOSSOMS THAT HANG ON THE BOUGH.

I do see my daughters briefly that summer. Our reunion is...cordial, yes, but not drenched in the joy I had so long envisioned. They do bear their father's stamp.

At word of *my* father's failing health, I hurry to London where I find the poor man gravely ill and his finances – not unexpectedly – a shambles. And as Mr. Butler – again not unexpectedly – fails to provide me a penny of support, I am back to earning a living. But not the stage. Dear Lord, not the stage.

(**FANNY** *rises, crosses to the book.*)

Before he became ill, my father earned a modest income giving public readings of William Shakespeare's plays in and about London. And now that he can no longer continue this enterprise, he bequeaths his annotated volumes to me.

And so I begin. Reading these glorious words. In school houses, libraries, concert halls, ballrooms. Most of my sponsors want only the more popular texts, but I refuse. Mr. Shakespeare composed a most significant canon of plays and I feel duty-bound to read each and every one. In succession. These readings console me as my father breathes his last. Sustain me through these years of separation as my daughters mature into women.

Sarah, at last, comes of age and is soon betrothed to a Pennsylvania physician. Owen Wister. Delightful man. Following the wedding, I begin reading Mr. Shakespeare here in America with amazing success. People too proper to darken the door of a theatre, flock to hear the notorious "Mrs. Kemble." And as I now perform all the parts in all the plays, my much celebrated Juliet is finally playing opposite an equally astounding Romeo!

Within a year Sarah gives birth to Owen, Junior, elevating me to the prestigious title of "grandmother." But my brightening hope for the future is soon eclipsed by a nation bent on War. "Civil" War. Harper's Ferry, Lincoln's election, Fort Sumter!

*(***PIANIST*** plays "Battle Hymn Of The Republic,"* [**MUSIC 18a – CIVIL WAR**]*)*

My former husband's operation of a leading slave plantation thrusts us into the heart of the conflict. Not surprisingly, our family is as divided as the nation: Sarah zealous for the North; Fan even more passionate for the South. My presence does little but exacerbate the tension, and so for peace – at least among ourselves – I sail, once again, for home. Where people talk of nothing but America's war! Speech after speech in Parliament urges recognition of the Confederacy!

(MEMBER OF THE HOUSE). Mr. Speaker! The Union's naval blockade is costing Great Britain a fortune!

(ANOTHER MEMBER OF THE HOUSE). To say nothing of jobs! Throwing in with the South means cotton for our mills!

(AND ANOTHER MEMBER OF THE HOUSE). Hear, hear! Slavery is America's problem not ours!

FANNY. One day I'm approached by an advocate of British neutrality. She knows of the journal I kept on the Butler plantation and suggests that if I, a woman who is held in great esteem, were to publish it...

(YOUNG FANNY). No, no, no! Out of the question! Making my journal public would be a violation of trust. My husband, why he would...

(A beat. She turns to the audience, smiles devilishly.)

FANNY. I hurry into my study and retrieve the heavy manuscript. Its pages are yellow, the ink faded, but in the very act of lifting it, I feel emboldened.

I have spent most of my life exiled to a world of illusion and lies. But this work. Its record is sound. Each observation, frank and true. But of course it is. Writing was my one great strength. This collection of scribbling. Here is my magic cloak. Here is my power.

In the spring of 1863, over the objections of Mr. Butler – my daughters – I submit: *Journal of a Residence on a Georgian Plantation* to the publisher. I have no way of knowing the book's impact on the outcome of America's war. But it is quite popular; more importantly, passages are read before that same wavering House of Parliament.

In the end, of course, Great Britain maintains her neutrality, the Union is preserved, and America's four million slaves are emancipated. Including those once owned by Mr. Pierce Butler...and me.

> **(THE PIANIST** *plays* **[MUSIC 19 – FINISH THE PLAY]** *softly.)*

Yes. Yes. Finish the play. Prospero, having cast a benumbing spell over his Royal prisoners, turns to Ariel.

(PROSPERO). Ariel, my spirit,

How fares the king and 's followers?

(ARIEL). Brimful of sorrow and dismay. Your charm so strongly works 'em that if you now beheld them, your affections would become tender.

(PROSPERO). Dost thou think so, spirit?

(ARIEL). Mine would, sir, were I human.

FANNY. "Mine would, sir, were I...human." These six words. "Mine would, sir, were I human." They soften Prospero, yes, but more, much more, they...

(She waves the thought away.)

(PROSPERO). And mine shall! Though with their high wrongs
I am struck to the quick, the rarer action, Ariel, is in
virtue than in vengeance! Go release them.

My charms I'll break, their senses I'll restore.

This rough magic I here abjure! I'll break my staff,

Bury it certain fathoms in the earth,

And deeper than did ever plummet sound

I'll drown my book.

FANNY. There we have it. Prospero has fully recovered the
power so savagely wrenched away years before. And,
as forgiveness is more the dominion of the strong than
the weak, he is now free, for the first time in all this
while, to absolve the past and finally let it...

Following the War, I remain in England and carry on
with my readings. My daughters write of their father,
his poor health, his lost fortune. Then, word arrives
that...Pierce Butler – having traveled south to rescue
his war-ravaged plantation – has contracted some local
disease and is...dead. The man is dead. Buried on his
tropical isle beneath the varnished evergreens and the
fanning gray moss.

I sail for America to offer my support. But Sarah is
inconsolable and Fan is off to Georgia and her father's
hallowed farms.

(Opening an imaginary envelope.)

What's this? I am invited to tour America's Wild
West! Pittsburgh, Cincinnati. Chicago. To read Mr.
Shakespeare's plays.

William Shakespeare! What shall I say of this, the
greatest English mind and heart? He was...

"Mine would, sir, were I human." William Shakespeare's
plays – all of them – are about one thing: being human.

Look at these characters. Hundreds and hundreds of them. And I am bound to each more intimately than mother to child. Night after night for almost a lifetime I walk in their shoes. Gaze through their eyes. Feel their innumerable emotions.

(She populates the stage with the ghosts of her art.)

FANNY.   I am Proteus, Valentine, Hamlet and Lear. Beatrice, Benedict, Macbeth and his Lady. Titania, Bottom; Malvolio and Belch. I am Emperor of Rome, Duke of Athens, Prince of Morocco. I am all the Kings of England from John One to Henry Eight. I am their queens, children, subjects.

I am Viola, Portia, Cordelia, Rosalind. Catherine of Aragon. Shylock, Iago, Cassius, Edmund. I am "Falstaff." I curse in verse!

My every speech coins words, mints maxims; I wallow like a puppy in puns!

Today I dig graves in Denmark; tomorrow I am queen of the Nile. I live in ancient Rome, Greece, Tunis, Cyprus. In fanciful worlds of nymphs and fairies. I am wed and divorced. Give birth and die.

Oh how I die! I am stabbed, stoned, beheaded, burned, drowned, bled, poisoned, starved, clubbed, hanged, suffocated. I swallow fiery coals; I am bitten by an asp.

Atheist, Muslim, Christian, Jew. Rake, drunkard, simpleton, hag. Insane, deformed, animal, corpse. My occupations leap from priest to prostitute; philosopher to fool; midwife to executioner.

(Dancing around the furniture.) Singer, dancer, minstrel, mime. Ghost, soothsayer, harpy and witch. I am patriot and traitor; victor and vanquished. I house mankind's highest aspirations, alongside his most heinous crimes.

(To the book.) I am all the "themes" that all the scholars of all time discover within these lines! And because I'm given to sentimentality, again and again and again, I fall in love!

(Fighting back the tears.) Mr. Shakespeare. He was my refuge, wasn't he? He...was my liberator.

Liberté.

> **(FANNY** *takes hold of the lectern. Her knees are weak. Painful. After a moment,* **THE PIANIST** *plays the single notes of* **[MUSIC 20 – LIBERTÉ: WHERE THE BEE SUCKS]. FANNY** *goes around to the book.)*

FANNY. Ariel enters with the King and his party; Caliban and his cohorts. Prospero turns to Antonio.

(PROSPERO). You, most wicked sir, whom to call brother
would even infect my mouth, I...do forgive
thy rankest fault.

FANNY. Dismissing Caliban, Prospero yanks back a curtain revealing Miranda and Ferdinand playing chess.

(MIRANDA). Sweet lord, you play me false!

(FERDINAND). No, my dear'st love, I would not for the world.

FANNY. Miranda looks up and sees the Royal Party.

(MIRANDA). O, WONDER! How beauteous mankind is!
O brave new world, that has such people in't!

(PROSPERO). 'Tis new to thee.

FANNY. Prospero turns to the King.

(PROSPERO). Sir, I invite your highness and your train
To my poor cell, where for this one night
I'll waste with...with the story of my life.
And in the morn to your ship and so to Naples,

(PROSPERO). Where I have hope to see the nuptial
 Of these our dear-beloved solemnized;
 And thence retire me to my Milan, where
 Every third thought shall be my grave.
 My Ariel?

   *(***FANNY*** turns to ***THE PIANIST***. *He stands.)*

FANNY. Chick... Calm seas and auspicious gales, that is thy charge.

   *(***THE PIANIST*** nods to her and sits. **FANNY** turns to the audience.)*

(PROSPERO). Then, to the elements, be free! And fare thou well!

   *(***FANNY*** watches **ARIEL** as he flies away. She extends her hand and waves to her devoted sprite. **THE PIANIST** plays a rousing finale, [MUSIC 20a – HAPPY ENDING]. **FANNY** suddenly snaps back. Dismisses the music.)*

FANNY. Yes, yes! The play has a happy ending. But remember, this is a world of illusion. For as the castaways sail for home, Prospero is pondering his death, Antonio remains unrepentant, and what kind of husband will Ferdinand make? We just now saw the fellow cheat at chess. Who knows what he will cheat at next?

Caliban, the abhorred slave. Now emancipated stands alone, abandoned on an island in the midst of a hostile sea.

(CALIBAN). FREEDOM, HEY-DAY! HEY-DAY...

FANNY. *(Looking over the stage she is about to leave forever.)* Freedom.

   (Taking a breath she turns to the audience.)

Now, like the shipwrecked survivors of our play, I depart this, my island of art and artifice, mystery and magic. Within the week I sail for home and the wedding of my daughter, Fan, to a James Wentworth Leigh. The man is not only an ordained member of the clergy, he is – in answer to my prayers – an Englishman.

After that, who knows what I'll do. Perhaps I'll...terrify my grandchildren with my memoirs:

Mrs. Kemble and her Fatal Legacy!

> (*She goes to the lectern and is about to read the epilogue, but stops. Closes the book. Walks down to the audience.* **THE PIANIST** *plays Mendelssohn's "Song Without Words, Op. 19, No. 6."*)

Now my charms are all o'erthrown,

And what strength I have's mine own,

Which is most faint: now, 'tis true,

I must be here confined by you,

Or sent to...England.

Let me not,

Since I have my dukedom got,

And pardon'd the deceiver, dwell

In this bare island by your spell;

Gentle breath of yours my sails

Must fill, or else my project fails,

Which was to please.

Now I want

Spirits to enforce, art to enchant,

And my ending is despair,

Unless I be relieved by prayer

Which pierces so that it assaults

Mercy itself and frees all faults.

FANNY. As you from crimes would pardon'd be,

Let your indulgence...set me...

Free.

>(**FANNY** *picks up the book, offers it to the audience for acknowledgment, bows to the* **PIANIST** *who bows back. She curtsies one last time and exits.*)

End of Play